ROOM 415

by Edward Lee
has been published in an edition of 452 copies
offered for sale in the following manner:

A fifty two copy, signed & lettered,
cloth hardcover edition.

A four hundred copy, signed & numbered,
limited edition chapbook.

Eel Lee

This is Number:

341

ROOM
415

EDWARD LEE

NECRO

2007

Room 415

Room 415 © 2004 by Edward Lee

Cover art © 2007 Travis Anthony Soumis
Travis would like to thank ahrum-stock.deviantart.com

This edition January 2007 © Necro Publications

First Edition Chapbook
ISBN: 1-889186-70-8

ROOM 415 is offered as a 400-copy signed and numbered limited edition softcover chapbook as well as a 52-copy signed and lettered limited edition hardcover.

Book Design & Typesetting:
David G. Barnett
faT caT Design

Cover Design:
David G. Barnett

Printing history: DAMNED: An Anthology of the Lost
[Deluxe Edition], April, 2004

Necro Publications
5139 Maxon Terrace
Sanford, FL 32771
www.necropublications.com

For: N–, Sh–, M–, He–, S–, Di–, Lynn, C–.

When Flood saw the naked woman in the window, he froze. He stood poised as a mannequin in the dark, lit cigarette in hand. Excitement flashed, first in his heart, then his groin. It was the spontaneity, he knew, the total surprise. From this angle (Flood was on the fifth floor, the woman down on the fourth) he couldn't see her face. Just a blur of shiny, ink-black hair, a flash of white breasts as she turned. Now she stood, back to window; his eyes locked on the lines of her shoulders, waist, hips. A perfect snow-white rump. At first he thought she must be wearing a white bikini, until a maintained stare revealed stark tanlines. *Another sun bunny,* Flood thought. After that first second of reaction, he shrugged, uninterested. *Why bother even looking?* he told himself. *What's the point?*

But he kept looking anyway. Was it boredom? Or hope?

A sheer, salmon-pink curtain billowed out the window. Flood's eyes remained on the buttocks and its perfect cleft, yet peripheral detail indicated that she was talking to someone. To her right, an unmade bed. Flood rubbed his crotch through boxer shorts—who could see? *It would at least be nice to get a look at the rest of her,* he complained. God, nature, or the universe could be mockingly cruel. The only reason he'd risen from bed and come to the window at all was to smoke. His secretary had booked him a non-smoking room, so he puffed before his own open window. He'd turned the a/c off; as a Seattlite, warm breezes coming off the water were a luxurious novelty, and so were all the inordinately attractive women he'd seen thus far walking down the streets, sitting in bars, and even shopping in grocery stores in string bikinis. Bikinis here seemed as commonplace as frumpish denim ankle-skirts and flannel blouses were on women in the Northwest. Flood didn't expect such a personal reaction. He'd traveled to cities all over the country whose women clearly outshone Seattle stock as far as looks were concerned. His boss, in fact, always bewailed sending him on these marketing trips, with comments like, "Sometimes it really sucks being the president of a big company, Jake."

"Why?"

"Because I gotta stay here and run the show, and send you guys to all these fancy hotels full of gorgeous babes."

Babes, Flood thought now. It didn't matter to him anymore.

He stood a moment further, smelling the fresh salt air. He looked straight out and could see only a vast darkness that seemed incalculable, even monstrous. An interesting acknowledgment: he couldn't see it but he knew it was there, the thousand-mile-long Gulf of Mexico.

His cigarette sizzled down, an orange brand; he glanced again to the window. The initial rush of voyeur's excitement had exited. Now the woman sat on the edge of the bed calmly fellating an apparent black man who stood before her with his slacks down. Flood noted that the slacks appeared to be high-quality, as did what appeared to be a black-silk shirt and black tie. Flood couldn't see the man's face. When Black Guy's hips began to flinch, he pushed the woman down on the bed and straddled her, silently masturbating the final moment.

The image raved. The woman's mouth gaped a greedy ecstasy, stark-white breasts atop the luxuriant tan; Flood thought of Hostess Snowballs topped by pink bon-bons. He was surprised by the clarity of detail he was able to see. Black Guy ejaculated viscid loops across the breasts, then shook out the last line across her lips. She sat back up to slowly suck out the endmost drops.

Another mindless rub to the crotch wrought no reaction. A masturbating voyeur's dream, yet Flood didn't care. His crotch felt comatose. *What a rip-off,* he thought to the sea.

For lack of nothing else, he lit another cigarette. He needn't be to the conference hall till noon, so he could sleep late. Besides, he really did enjoy this secret existential luxury: being totally alone before the lightless face of nature. Flood was sales director for a company that made wireless computer components; hence, these electronics shows proved a necessity to travel out of

Seattle. His firm, in fact, had achieved a cutting-edge rep in the field. He'd always been successful but never more than now. Fifty, and he was living the white-collar success story: close to a mid-six-figure salary, stock options that guaranteed a lavish retirement, waterfront home on Puget Sound. 100k in his savings account, and a Mercedes *and* a Cadillac.

Yet Flood felt poor as a vagabond.

Felicity had wed the man she'd been cheating with immediately after the divorce, so at least there was no alimony. They'd been married for ten years, and he supposed, now, that she'd cheated on him for as long. He even knew she was a gold-digger but he didn't care (Flood had lots of gold); he simply loved her for all he was worth, her flaws, her flirting drug problems, and her lack of character, and all else. She was more beautiful than any woman he'd known, and she soon became the very seat of his desire.

Oh, God. What a wreck my life is...

He knew he shouldn't think about her; Dr. Untermann warned him of such pitfalls. What had she called his disorder? "A thematic-erotic inversion, Mr. Flood. It's a fairly commonplace sexual dysfunction. A stimulating image or situation ignites an instantaneous and very normal sexual response. But then the inversion sets in. Stimulation reminds you of your ex-wife, and your ex-wife nearly destroyed your life. Let me put it this way, Mr. Flood, in more comprehensible terms. Your married life can be likened to a car wreck. You're a crashed car. You're going to be in the shop for awhile."

Analogy notwithstanding, finally he understood,

to the chagrin of his sex drive. Any woman who excited him would dig up memories of Felicity, then all bets were off.

Shit! His cigarette had burned down in his musing, burning his fingers. He pitched it out the window and watched the ember fall five stories in total silence.

That silence, and the darkness, seemed a comfort here. It honed off his edges. Uncaring now, he glanced down at the fourth-floor window again, spotted the ink-haired girl on hands and knees on the bed. A wide, stocky white man with a shaved head was taking her from behind, quite frenetically. He'd dropped his slacks, and as he humped her, shrugged out of his own silk shirt, a deep maroon. The bald head shined. The wide back was astonishingly hairy; it reminded Flood of a professional wrestler. Flood focused down…

What happened next was easily discerned in spite of the distance and angle. The bald man's head dipped down, whereupon he spat between the girl's buttocks, then pulled his penis out—

"Hey!" Flood could hear the girl's sudden disapproval. "I told you you couldn't—"

Then a sharp yelp.

The bald man had thumbed open her buttocks and slammed his penis into her rectum.

He humped even more frenetically now, grasping her hips close to restrain her objection. In a moment the thrusts slowed, then stopped.

The night air carried stray words upward, which Flood could hear with little trouble:

"Leon! Oscar put it in my—"

"*Damn* it, Oscar! That hurts!"

"—I told him he couldn't put—"

The bald man was gruffly wiping his penis off on some fabric, presumably the girl's dress.

"Leon! Tell Oscar not to do—"

"Shut up, hosebag—"

She whirled around, sitting upright on the bed. "Don't you call me a—"

SLAP!

Flood flinched at what he witnessed. The bald man—Oscar, evidently—had one arm back into his silk shirt when his hand blurred. He cracked an open palm hard against her face.

First, silence. Then—

"You can't hit me!"

"Be quiet, Jinny," a third voice said.

More silence.

Flood calculated, something he was good at. *The girl's Jinny, the bald guy Oscar. The third voice must be Leon, the black guy.* Flood continued to watch and listen.

"What do you wanna do with this cum-drain, Leon?" Oscar said.

"Leon, tell him not to talk to me like that!"

SLAP!

Flood flinched again. Leon the Black Guy calmly walked back into view: tall, lean, well-groomed.

"You don't like it when Oscar talks to you with disrespect?"

Jinny was sobbing now through obvious stinging pain. "Nuh-no!"

"Then why do you treat *me* with disrespect?"

Now the silence gaped.

The girl looked up wanly as Leon and Oscar towered over her.

"Whuh-what do you mean?"

"Don't insult me, Jinny. I've always taken care of you, and now you betray me."

"I-I never…"

"You're made, bitch," Oscar said, his bald head out of frame. "You're busted."

"We know, Jinny. So admit it. If you admit it, then everything'll be cool. If you don't… Just, please—don't insult me."

Flood's eyes were peeled now, the drama cutting through the dark. More words flew upward, like tiny bats.

"I-I worked a car show in Tampa luh-luh-last weekend…"

Flood could see Leon standing, arms crossed, his head, too, out of frame.

"Um-hmm. And?"

The girl's lower lip quivered, one cheek a blushing pink from the slaps. "And—that's all."

"Solo? Or were you working for Henry Phipps?"

"Solo!" she nearly jumped up and exclaimed.

"Hmm? Really?"

"Yes! I swear!"

"I've lost three girls to Henry. I'm not going to lose anymore. I won't let you girls embarrass me like that. I take care of you all, and I don't deserve to be humiliated."

"I was soloing the car show, I swear to God! I wasn't working on the side for Phipps!"

"I heard she was," Oscar said.

"I wasn't! I swear, I swear!"

Leon: "What do you think, Osc? You believe her?"

"No. Lemme fuck her up. Lemme bottle-job her."

Jinny put face in hands, sobbing. "I didn't, I didn't. I'd never work for someone else…"

"I…," Leon began. A beat. A gust of breeze. Then: "I believe her."

Now her sobs were of relief.

"Thank you for being honest, Jinny. I hope we can maintain a wonderful friendship and working relationship."

"Thank you, thank you. I made about a grand, I'll give it all to you tomorrow."

"Not necessary. I know you need it for your child. But you know the rules. If you hadn't told the truth, it would be…much worse. Right? You know the rules?"

She gulped and nodded.

"Do you deserve what's coming?"

Another gulp, another nod.

"Good girl. I've always liked you. You can make it hard, or you can make it easy."

The girl stood up, head stooped, her nudity lusterless now.

Oscar seemed to be putting something on his hand. Flood's mind flashed with the worst possibilities (*Brass knuckles? A blackjack?*) but then he noticed it was a glove, a large black glove. The girl turned to face Oscar, while Leon chicken-winged her from behind.

"Don't make a sound," he said into her ear.

By now Flood realized the glove's uniqueness: it was a sand-mitt, something police and prison guards used as a non-lethal weapon.

Holy shit, he thought.

In the dark he reached for the phone to call hotel security and report an assault, but—

The room's darkness around him, and the glaring image from the lit window, made him feel encased in cement.

"Not the face," Leon said, propping the girl up by her elbows.

Oscar opened and closed the gloved hand, smacked it into his palm several times.

Call security, Flood thought.

The bald man belly-punched her once with a sound like a sandbag hitting the floor.

WHAP.

She tried to double over but Leon's hold wouldn't permit it.

WHAP. Another jab to the belly. Then another, and another.

The legs she stood on gave way; Leon kept holding her up, like a trainer holding a boxing pad. The fifth blow to the belly sent her head bouncing around, a ball on a spring. She must barely be conscious now.

Call the police! Flood screamed at himself, hand hovering over the phone.

His mind, somehow, felt vacant, his spirit... gone.

Then his hand drifted off on its own...

Confusion consumed him. Flood's eyes were riveted to the window. He kept watching the brutality, knowing he should do something to help the girl, but his conscience was nowhere to be found. Oscar afforded her several more blows to the belly, then threw her down on the bed. Both men walked out of view. Jinny shuddered on the mattress in a fetal position, gasping, pain stamped into her face like a twisted mask.

God Almighty, Flood thought. *What am I doing?*

Without even any direct awareness, Flood had pulled his shorts down and was masturbating. His penis felt alien, the erection so hard and so complete, for a moment he didn't believe it was his own. A final stare, then, at the girl's brutalized nakedness, the suffering on her face...

Fresh sensations churned, then exploded; Flood nearly cried out when his orgasm broke, gusts from his groin shooting feet-long plumes of sperm through the air. The first spurts actually sailed out the window, and what was left pelted the wall. Flood collapsed.

This was a big deal to him—his first orgasm in three years.

《《—》》

Next morning, his confusion turned to shame. *How could that have happened?* he asked his own face in the bathroom mirror. *What kind of a person am I?*

He contemplated that question for the short walk

across Gulf Boulevard to the convention center. And he *knew*. *I'm not a bad person. I don't exploit people, or lie, or cheat, or steal.* So what had happened last night?

Flood's job at the electronics show was essentially information support: to explain marketing and sales details to any prospective high-volume buyers, which generally didn't occur until the last day. His underlings ran the booth while he wandered the showroom, pretending to be checking out the competition's new products—*pretending* because his mind was surely elsewhere. He wended through the crowd, oblivious and still shaken; he scarcely even noticed the human eye-candy that some booths sported: stunningly beautiful women in bikinis and high-heels, handing out brochures. Additionally, when competitors he knew personally bid him a greeting he could only wave back or nod in the dimmest fog. Flood felt like a single bug in a haystack.

Walking around for several hours didn't clear his head as he'd hoped. *I should have called the police immediately, or the security desk—something, anything. But what did I do instead? I stood there and jerked off because I haven't been able to come since Felicity left me. I witnessed a girl getting beaten, and instead of doing anything about it...I JERKED OFF! What the hell is WRONG with me?* It didn't matter that it was just a few belly-punches; it was brutal and it was sick. It was a criminal assault. The situation had been easy enough to figure, nearly a cliche: "Leon" was obviously the pimp, "Oscar" the lieutenant, and Jinny the prostitute. She'd been holding out on Leon, working on the side behind his back—a supreme no-no in the field. Flood's id kicked in a plea to rationalize: *Okay, yeah, sure, she got beat up, but that happens to dishonest whores. It's part of the turf and she knows it. She's a whore, and prostitution is illegal. Leon and the bald guy are panderers, and pandering is illegal. They're all a bunch of criminals, so why do I feel guilty? I'M not a criminal. If they saw someone beating ME up, would THEY call the police? Fat chance. So I'm not gonna let myself feel like shit because a girl who had it coming to her got her ass kicked...*

Flood felt better for all of five minutes, then slumped again when he admitted the falsehood.

By three, the convention center had become a hive; he thought of the floor of the New York Stock Exchange, the only difference being that the floor of the New York Stock Exchange didn't have voluptuous women in bikinis prancing about. That voluptuousness, though, only depressed him more. It was for everyone else but...

Not for me. Never for me.

Last night was an anomaly; he knew he was back to square one. His penis felt like a flap of numb skin in the trousers.

I don't need to be here, he realized. *Let the young guys have at it. I think I'll go get drunk.*

"How's business, fellas?" he asked his sales staff back at his company's booth.

"We're kicking ass," said Farris, their Tom Cruise lookalike technical rep, who then held up a clipboard, "and taking names."

"Good work," Flood said, impressed by the list of possible buyers. "You guys are hauling them in."

The sales rep, Nathans, looked more like John Candy than Cruise. He glanced up just as a competitor's ad girl walked by: hourglass figure bursting out of a vermillion string bikini, the top of which hoisted what must have been 38 double-D's. A big Colegate grin flashed behind the sign she held, advertizing network-user docking stations for palmtop computers. The sign read DOCK WITH ME!

"We're hauling them in all right, boss," Nathans remarked. "But I wouldn't mind if we had a couple ad-girls like that."

"We don't need tits and ass to sell our peripherals," Flood said. "Ours work, theirs don't."

"Yeah, but still…"

The leering grins of both of the younger men followed the sultry woman. From behind, the tanned rump jiggled, cellulite-free, each perfect buttock totally nude, divided only by a t-back strap.

"How'd you like to plug something into *her* ethernet slot, huh, Nathans?" Farris asked under his breath.

Nathans made a ludicrous pelvic gesture. "Yeah, seven and a half gigs of RAM."

Everything is sex, came Flood's dismal concession. At least he was conditioned now—yes, last night was indeed a fluke. The vision of the woman did little for him.

Flood tried to mask his despair. "Fellas, you know what I'm gonna do?"

"Give us a raise?" Nathans guessed.

"One better. I'm gonna leave you guys here to work your asses off while I go walk on the beach. You wanna know *why* I'm gonna do that?"

"Because you *can*?" Farris said.

"Smart boy."

"No problemo, boss," Farris assured. "We've got it covered. Put your faith in us."

Nathans piped in, "Aw, that's his kiss-the-boss's-ass way of saying we don't need you."

"Works for me," Flood replied. "I'll be here all day tomorrow to handle those sales interviews. Anything you guys need before I blow this computer-geek pop stand?"

"Maybe just a collar and chain," Farris said.

Flood looked quizzical. "A collar and chain?"

"Yeah, to keep Nathans off that docking-station bimbo in the t-back."

"Don't need it now," Nathans told them. "I already shot my load in my pants the last time she came around."

"See ya, boss!"

"Have fun on the beach!"

Flood walked away, shaking his head. *Kids,* he thought. *If they only knew.* He hustled out of the con center, but even crossing the street back to his hotel, his vision was further assailed by more of the same imagery: more young women in bikinis strutting up and down the sidewalk, sashaying across the parking lots, bending over their open car trunks to lift out beach towels and coolers. *Holy Jesus,* Flood's thoughts groaned. *I can't turn my head without seeing it...*

He all but raced back up to his room, frustrations piling up. *Oh, man,* he thought when he looked in the bathroom mirror after changing. *Gee, I wonder if anyone'll guess I'm not from Florida.* Parrot-green swim trunks, clunky Seattle sandals, and skin whiter than a Kenmore refrigerator. He slipped on an old Mariners shirt, sighing, and left the room.

More young women in bikinis stood waiting for the elevator, chatting gayly. One girl's bikini—a bright and nearly luminous fuchsia—clung so tightly to her breasts and rump that it seemed painted on her. Another had nipples which poked out like thumb-ends. Flood felt a twinge in his chest, turned, and fled for the stairs. Better to walk the five flights than stand waiting in that gaggle of cruel reminders.

He felt calmer once in the cool stairwell. 4TH FLOOR, read the next door down. Flood stalled. *What am I doing?* he asked himself. His hand was turning the knob.

He *knew* what he was doing.

Morbid curiosity, I guess… What did he expect? To actually *see* the girl? What was her name? Jinny? *What, I think I'm just going to SEE HER walking out of the room?*

He pushed his confusion behind. In his mind, he pictured the hotel's eye-beam configuration, then turned on the next wing.

That must be it, he realized. Last room on the south wing.

415, the door read.

A plastic tag in the key-card slot let him know: DO NOT DISTURB.

So this was the room. Room 415. *Big deal,* he thought. But at least the unspecified curiosity that had brought him was sated now.

"Are chew lookink for Meester Kingston, sir?"

The voice startled Flood to the extent that he almost shouted. A Latino accent, Cuban probably. He caught his breath and turned to face a chubby housemaid with brown hair back in a bun standing behind a cart full of brooms, towels, etc. Mammoth plops of breasts looked jello-like in the blasé work apron. Before Flood could answer, she continued the prattle: "Because if chew are, chew must call him, not knock. See the sign, hmm? Meester Kingston never wanna be bothered. He good man, teep good to all of us. He always get theese room here when he here."

Information overload. *She must mean Leon, the black guy,* Flood put together. *And he's a regular, probably brings his stable here whenever there's a nearby convention.* Finally Flood got his brain back on track. "Oh, no, I'm sorry. Stupid me; I got off on the wrong floor. I'm on the fifth."

Her breasts tremored when she bent to pick up a can of Comet. "Well, yes, but theese is forf floor, sir."

"Yes, yes, I just realized that. Have good day," and then he offered a covering smile and walked for the elevator.

Jesus, what an idiot! But he wasn't even to the elevator cove when he heard the door open.

He stepped up his pace. *Fuck!* But what was he anxious about? Leon Kingston had never seen Flood before, and there's no way he or his cohort could know what he'd witnessed last night.

Flood wisely didn't turn when his ears picked up the voice he'd already heard: "Maria, good afternoon!"

"Good afternoon to chew too, Meester Kingston."

"And how are you today? Muy buena, I hope."

A blushing chuckle. "Very muy buena, sir."

Flood turned into the cove, hit the down button. In dread he could almost hear what she might say: *Strange gringo man was standink in-frunna chore door,* but then he relaxed at her real words after obviously accepting a tip. "Muchas gracias, sir!"

Hurry, hurry, he shot the thought at the elevator. The carpeted hallway would betray no footsteps. He still didn't know what he was afraid of, though; to Leon Kingston the Pimp, Flood was just another pale-skinned tourist. The elevator hadn't opened yet when two figures came around the corner.

Flood nodded, smiled.

"Good afternoon, sir," came Leon's upbeat greeting. He looked better than Flood's stereotypes imagined. Ring-like Billy-Dee-Williams hair, sharp conservative dark slacks and a fine heather-gray silk shirt, open at the neck but no gaudy gold pimp chains. Class, not flash. "I hope you're enjoying your stay at the Rosamilia."

"I-I am," Flood said, off guard. "Very much. It's a gorgeous hotel." The weirdest impulse, then, just another curiosity, a test to elicit a response. "I take it you're one of the managers here?"

"No, no, sir. But it's my favorite hotel on the beach. I always stay here during convention weeks."

"Oh, really? The CES convention? That's where I'm at."

"All of them, sir. Leon Kingston. Very pleased to meet you."

Flood shook the firm, long-fingered black hand. *Wow, he ducked that one well, but what did I expect him to say? I'm a pimp?* "Jake Flood. If you're looking for the best wireless peripherals, stop by my booth across the street."

"I just might do that, sir, I just might. Mr. Flood, please meet my good friend—"

Only at that moment did Flood notice Leon's companion: elegant-physique'd, slender yet well-curved, hair radiant and black as ink cut straight as a bezel edge at the collarbone line—

"—Jinny," Leon finished.

Flood surprisingly didn't falter. He shook the cool soft hand, and said "Hello, Jinny," then noted her fine, high-cheek-boned face and runway-model poise. The paprika-red wrap-dress clung to her curves as if she'd just been fitted by a pro fashion consultant. Flood's earlier presumption was clarified; she was *not* a tacky convention whore, but an upper-end call-girl.

"Hello," she said, smiling meekly. Then she seemed to restrain an uncomfortable flinch. "It's nice to meet you."

"First time on St. Pete Beach, Mr. Flood?"

The image of the girl stunned him once he compared it to the image he remembered last night:

sperm all over her, face stamped into a mask of pain as she lay doubled-over on the bed, trim belly darkening with fresh bruises. "I-uh, yes, it is. Really nice beach town, nothing at all like Lauderdale and South Beach." He tried to sound conversational, if only for an excuse to pay more visual attention to Jinny, a truly beautiful woman. "At my age, I like things a little laidback, a little less rowdy."

"*Your* age?" Leon interjected. "I'm forty-five, Mr. Flood, and I *know* you're younger than me."

A pimp being ingratiating, Flood suspected, but he did know that he still looked good for the Big Five Oh. Before he could think of a reply, Leon continued, "But you could use a little sun, Mr. Flood, if you don't mind my saying so. Give me three guesses. Seattle, Portland, or…"

"Got it on first one," Flood admitted, but thinking simultaneously: *What a pillar of character I am. I'm having a congenial conversation with a brutal PIMP. Good job, Flood. You're a real gem.* At the edges of his vision he noted Jinny's forced smile, her continued repression of the pain at her abdomen. *I should have called the cops on this criminal....* "And, no, we don't get much sun there. In fact I was on my way out for a walk on the beach right now."

"Great day for it. Lots of great bars and restaurants on this beach." Like a magic trick, a business card appeared in Leon's fingers. "And just in case you're interested—since this is your first time—feel free to call my service number, if you'd like a top-notch tour guide to show you around."

Flood looked at the card. SUN & SAND TOUR

GUIDES - LEON KINGSTON, DIRECTOR, and a number. *Tour guides, huh?* Flood thought. *Smooth, very smooth.*

Flood couldn't believe the illogic of his next words. "Is, uh, is Jinny one of your guides?"

"Indeed, she is, Mr. Flood, but unfortunately Jinny's feeling under the weather today—"

Yeah, I'll bet she is... "Oh, I'm sorry," Flood expressed to her. His eyes couldn't quite meet hers. "Catch a cold or something?" he asked for no other reason than to sound nonchalant.

Finally her hands came to her abdomen. "No, just one of those twenty-four-hour stomach bugs—"

"—but I'd be delighted to introduce you to one of our other guides, and I guarantee you, Mr. Flood, they're all just as provocative as Jinny," and with that, Leon shot Flood a quick wink.

So this is how it works here, Flood thought. Since Felicity, he'd hired more than one "escort" girl, and in the end, it was all a waste of time and money.

The elevator opened, then they were going down.

"Maybe I'll give you a call tomorrow after the convention." Flood slipped the card into his wallet. "But for now, I think I'll just have a leisurely stroll on the beach. Thanks for the card, though."

"My pleasure, Mr. Flood," Leon finished up. "Enjoy the beach."

"I will. Nice meeting you both."

Jinny made another nod and pained smile, while Leon's own smile followed him out of the elevator into the atrium.

Jesus, Flood thought. *Some bag of worms.* He

made for the courtyard which would lead to the hotel's own beach bar, but stalled when he reached for his cell phone. *Damn it.* He'd left it in his room, and he really needed to check his voice mail for the Seattle office. A queue of loud women in bikinis piled into the elevator cove, chattering, so Flood said *To hell with going back up,* and turned into a nicely paneled anteroom containing several payphones with private booths. He zipped in his credit card, was about to dial, when voices interrupted.

"Shit, Leon, I really hurt."

"Well, I hope you learned your lesson."

"I did but I still *hurt.* Oscar didn't have to hit me that hard."

"Osc wanted to hit you a lot harder, and would have if I'd told him too. Instead of giving me lip, try being grateful."

It's them, Flood realized. They must be in one of the other booths and left the door ajar. Flood's was ajar too.

"When's Oscar taking me home?"

"When you finish blowing me. So shut up and do it."

Flood held the dead phone to his ear, feigning use, but sat tensed, listening.

Moments of silence ticked by, then Leon grunted and said, "Yeah, yeah—shit. Slow now, suck it all out…" More silence. "No, no. Swallow… Good girl."

Love in the afternoon, Flood thought.

"Osc took a couple girls to the Tradewinds Resort for that pilot conference. He'll be here in a couple hours, then he'll take you home."

"Leon, I need a vykie. Bad."

"One, and that's it."

"*Leon!* I *really hurt!* Please, gimme one for tonight, too. *Please.*"

"Jesus, Jinny, you're gonna turn into a junkie like Ann and Therese."

"I can barely even *walk.* Oscar was hitting me so hard it felt like a sledgehammer."

"You girls take too much of this shit…"

Vykie, Flood thought. He'd read about it: Vicadin, the prescription pain-killers, a morphine derivative. Popular street drug now.

"Ann's supposed to meet me here for dinner," Leon remarked. "Didn't see her at all last night. Did you?"

"Yeah, but just for a minute."

"How'd she do?"

"Said she did one-hour tricks all day, then bagged an all-nighter with some rich guy from Maryland. And she said she needs more vykies."

"I already gave her enough. You girls gotta watch it with that shit, I been telling you. Now come on. Let's go to the bar and get some lunch, then you can wait for Oscar. You feeling better now?"

"Yes. Thank you."

The door clattered open. Flood faked dialing the phone; in the corner of an eye he saw Leon and Jinny leave the anteroom, none the wiser of his presence.

Very, very interesting, he thought. *A day in the life of a pimp and prostitute.* Flood dialed for real, found no messages in wait, then left.

Now he got to thinking. How many of the beautiful women here were really call-girls? Everywhere he looked, they sat, walked, or waited. *Why should I care?* he asked himself. *Whether they're hookers or not, I can't do anything with them anyway.* He kept mental blinders on walking through the resort's pool area, ignoring side-glimpses of more, more, more drop-dead-gorgeous women in the sparsest bikinis, all sprawled out on lounge chairs like things on deliberate display. *You'd think I'd be used to this by now, cauterized.* When did learned behavior sink into the psyche permanently? After three years? Flood wished it were so, wished that all desire would just die.

The hotel's beach bar was just as bad, preeminent breasts maximized by so many women sitting at tables, leaning over fruity drinks. The bar was sufficient but too busy. Flood wanted to find a remote place, where he could think…

He embarked to the beach, clunky Seattle sandals sinking in sugar-white sand. The nearly wave-free Gulf of Mexico looked more like a vast and very tranquil lagoon. *This is better… Tone down, relax. Get your mind off things….* Like—

Last night…

What had come over him? He'd chosen a sexual self-indulgence over a typical civic duty, as if his orgasm was more important than a woman being beaten. *Get off it!* he suddenly yelped at himself.

Oh, no, he thought next.

The mental blinders weren't working out here. Lines of them: women with faces and bodies worthy of swimwear calendars. *God in heaven! Stop!*

The woman seemed to drift rather than walk down the beach; it seemed as though she were an entity coming out of the sun. Flood's heart shimmied even at the initial distance, eyes blooming at this virtual paragon bereft of defect. Waist-length hair the color of the same sun-lit sand she walked on danced in the faint breeze coming off the Gulf. Zero body fat but every contour full, even exploited for the visual effect. Breasts the size and undoubted firmness of fresh grapefruits. A harder cardiac shimmy when he noted in detail her apparel: a white fishnet bikini, each "box" of which was one inch square, and through these boxes *everything* was flaunted. Beer-can-top-sized areolae, darkly puckered, and nipple-ends sticking out as hard and crisply delineated as bullet cartridges: perfect cylinders of pink flesh. His gaze trembled to the pubic region, where the large fishnet squares made no secret of the fact that she dealt with an expert electrolysist, the vaginal furrow and mystical folds simply right *there,* for all to see, burgeoning against the threads.

God's really kicking my ass today—showing me THIS, Flood thought. His groin seemed to cringe. The woman appeared to be in a hurry, looking over her shoulder. Flood just stood there; he didn't even bother trying to *pretend* he wasn't staring overtly at her body.

She walked right up, stopped; she seemed perturbed but cheerily greeted him. "Hi."

"Huh-hi," Flood said.

She kept looking behind her. A gust of wind lifted her white-blond hair. Flood was staring at the nipples showing through the net squares but managed to be coherent enough to ask, "Is something wrong?"

"Well, yeah. Some filthy old drunk guy is following me…"

It pained him, but he took his eyes off her body and looked down the beach. In the distance, he saw a guy with glasses staring back but he wasn't moving. He was just standing there staring as no doubt many, many men stared at her with regularity. Dressed like this—if one could call a few ounces of threads "dress"—she must be used to it.

"No, not him. That guy."

Flood's eyes flicked. The glare of sun provided a momentary camouflage…then, from its glow a man emerged. *You gotta be kidding me,* Flood thought. It was one of those beach denizens, who was probably forty-five but looked sixty-five. Raggy shorts and flip-flops, skin scorched by decades in the sun, skinny but with a belly sticking out from chronic liver damage.

"Does this guy even have teeth?" Flood remarked. "He looks like Captain Salty on the skids."

The girl laughed but was still addled. "He's been following me for a half mile, saying the dirtiest things, stuff like because of my bikini I'm asking for it."

"Yeah, well, I think all this guy's gonna be asking for real soon is a liver transplant. Look at him. He's a wreck."

The man staggered closer. Tufts of matted hair

sprouted around the rim of a crooked Orioles cap stained nearly white with salt from sweat. The gray-blond beard looked like fungus-encrusted Brillo. "Hey, there, brother," he cragged, "what say let's double-team that honey? You see the tits and box on that?"

Flood snapped, very unlike him, and stuck his face right in the old man's, shouting, "What the FUCK is your problem, you wasted geezer? I mean besides the obvious alcohol problem? What are you doing harassing that woman?"

Captain Salty didn't back down. "Don't'cha be messing' with me, brother, unless ya want more'n ya can handle. Get out my way so's I can make me some time with that piece'a splittail—"

Flood clouted the man once on the forehead, so hard his fist came away aching. That was it for Captain Salty. He was out cold, flat on his back.

"That's so *great!*" the girl squealed.

Flood was shocked at himself. Several couples sitting on beach towels applauded.

"Well…I guess he had it coming," Flood said.

"It's about time somebody cleaned that guy's clock," a man in a fold-up chair said, and a beautiful woman next to him, in a raving pink thong, added, "He's out here every day, running his gutter-mouth, and staring at people."

The remarks made Flood feel better for his violence. The girl in the fishnet took his arm. "Come on. Let me buy you a drink."

"No, really, that's not necessary—"

"Come on," she insisted.

Now he felt self-conscious, ludicrous even in his parrot-green trunks and stark-white skin.

"Thank you," she said. "That guy was creeping me out."

"I can imagine. I'm not a violent person but sometimes—I don't know—I have no tolerance for sloppy, dirty, loud-mouthed drunks."

"This is usually a nice, low-key beach. People come out here to mind their own business and have a nice time, but every now and then you'll run into some guy like that who ruins things for everyone." Her right arm clasped Flood's left, while her fingers smoothed over his forearm. It almost seemed affectionate, and that titillated him since he'd had no genuine affection for a very long time, or…perhaps not ever. Even during his marriage, when it seemed stable, he knew now that Felicity's affection had been a play-act. Her only real affection she'd saved for the men she was seeing behind his back. Nevertheless, *this*…was nice. In his swim trunks he could feel his cock filling with desire and blood—rare for him. Butterflies fluttered in his stomach.

"Well, I'm just really grateful for what you did," she was going on. "I work this beach sometimes twice a month, and I'm *always* running into that guy."

Flood was distracted. Impulse kept dragging his eyes to catch glimpses of the net-covered breasts, the bare nipples extruding. *Oh, Jesus, this is crazy…* But what had she said? "Maybe that guy learned his lesson, that if he's gonna act like an ass, sometimes he's gonna get decked. But what did you mean when you said—"

She obviously already knew the question; perhaps the remark was her lead-in. "I work this beach, and others. Resort areas, tourist beaches, and especially conventions. I'm a tour guide. My name's Carol. What's yours?"

A *tour guide*? "Jake," Flood answered her. "I'm a computer accessory salesman from Seattle."

She giggled, a vocal gesture drenched in sex. She stopped, turned, and ran a hand down his white arm. "Believe me, I could tell you're not from here. Be careful, you'll burn fast."

Honey, I'm already burning.

"So I won't jack you around with the usual games. I'm a call-girl, Jake, one of the higher-priced kind." She stood and coyly ran a toe across the sand, making squiggles. "I charge a lot by most standards but—"

"You're worth it," he said without thinking. He laughed to himself. "This sounds corny, and I'm sure you hear it all the time, but you're absolutely the most beautiful woman I've ever seen."

Carol blushed. Now a finger made circles on his chest, through the V of his open shirt. Flood felt his own nipples instantly stand up, as his eyes struggled not to stare outright at hers. When she opened her hand and ran her palm inside his shirt, Flood's penis began to drool, threatening to spring up to full hardness right in his trunks.

"You're sweet, thank you. My rates are high, but because of what you did for me back there, I'll give you a half-rate for anything, I mean, if you're interested."

"I—" was all Flood could say.

"No pressure, and if you don't want to, that's cool. Just think about it."

"I—"

"Come on! Let's get a drink!"

She was dragging him off again. The situation was so cliched: middle-aged workaholic walking arm in arm with a stunning bombshell, feeling like he was real again. It *wasn't* real at all, but that didn't matter.

Their hips bumped as they walked, each bump urging another drop of pre-ejaculant down his urethra. When the tanned skin of her thigh slid against his, he could've moaned.

"I love this bar. Wanna know why?"

"Good drink specials?"

"No! It's outrageously overpriced! But I love it 'cos it's always empty!"

"That's more my speed too," Flood said for lack of an intelligent response.

"I'm supposed to meet my friend Therese here later."

The name crackled in his head. *Therese.* From his eavesdrop on Leon and Jinny. *Jesus, Jinny,* Leon had complained, *you're gonna turn into a junkie like Ann and Therese.* Vicadin, they'd been talking about: needle-free heroin. But it was clear Carol couldn't be into similar recreations, not with a body and glow like this. She didn't really even look like a prostitute: she looked too grand for that, too perfect.

The bar sprawled before a long, massive swimming pool, before an even more massive pink hotel that looked more like a castle. The elegant edifice threw a football-field sized shadow onto the beach.

No customers at the bar, nor at any of the umbrella'd tables on the bar's flank. This "worked" for Flood, indeed, for at any moment his arousal would be plain to see. An attractive fiftyish woman polished a glass and smiled at them.

"Tequila Moonrise, and whatever my friend's having," Carol said. Flood ordered a Beck's draft.

"And I told you, this is on me," Carol insisted. "I can't afford to eat here, but I can always swing a few drinks."

"I'd be more than happy to p—"

"Hush!"

The drinks arrived. A menu shaped like a scallop shell was placed before them, then the barmaid curtly walked away.

"Wow. Lobster Fritters," Flood commented of the menu. Twenty-two bucks for four.

"They're great but way overpriced. One time I had them, though, and they're delicious. A j—" She stalled. "A client got them for me."

She was going to say a john, Flood realized. "Let's get some. I'm buying. I'm buying everything."

"Jake, come on, I said this was my treat."

"Won't hear of it. And besides—" He looked at her and nearly rolled his eyes in awe. "Where on earth are you carrying money, anyway? I know it's not stashed in that top."

She giggled again, raised her other hand, which brandished a minuscule fleshtone wrist-purse. She zipped it open and slipped him a business card. "If you're not interested now, maybe you will be later. But just so you know, I'm a grand for all night, and that's anything you want, as many times as you can get off. Five hundred for an hour, and two for a blow. But for you, half off."

Flood looked at the card. Because she'd mentioned Therese after Leon's reference to her, he expected the card to be identical to the one Leon had given him, but instead, this one read: SUN ANGELS TOUR GUIDES - HENRY PHIPPS, MNGR. He remembered the Phipps' name...

Leon's competition...

The side of her calf touched his. She chatted her background, which sounded typical and very non-harrowing. It was small-talk, it was meaningless, and Flood knew that given her profession, *he* was meaningless. He was to her what a potential network buyer was to Flood. Once they said "no, thanks," they were reduced to insignificance. But none of this mattered. She was doing her job with artistry, making him feel at ease and covertly stimulating him with her cheery voice, her giggles, her eye gestures and body language. Flood was enjoying her company, and she hadn't been lying. There was never any pressure. "Those were delicious," she said of the lobster fritters. Flood had also ordered satay, fresh-water shrimp skewers, and lastly, oysters on the half-shell.

"Oh, I love raw oysters. You read my mind!" A hot hand opened on his thigh when she whispered, "And it's true what they say. They really do make me horny!"

Flood smiled. *I'm sure they do. She's working me, all right... and I don't care.*

His breath thinned when he watched her eat, daintily holding up the shell, the tip of her tongue slipping around the oyster. Then she sucked it all right into her mouth.

Oh, God...

And now her gestures became less covert: her hand smoothing over his thigh, her legs rubbing his more directly. "Relax," she whispered next. "She's way over there, and can't see under the bar anyway..."

"What?" Flood began, then gritted his teeth. He tensed when her fingers slipped under his shirt and worked their way into the waistband of his trunks. His balls drew up at once, and even before her hand was on it, his penis shot fully hard. His first social instinct was to pull her hand out—*Someone might see!*—but why care?

"Relax, relax." Her whisper was like hot liquid. "There's no one here. Let me play with it..."

She knew how to play. Her fingers slipped all around, so lightly at first his nerves barely registered the tactility, then with a smooth firmness. Each beat of Flood's heart forced more blood upward, to the extent that his already erect penis seemed to lengthen, by force.

"What do you think?" she whispered.

He could barely talk. "I-can't. You don't understand—it-it won't work. I-I-I can never come. I can never keep it up..."

Her hand gripped the shaft like a flight-stick, the pad of her thumb twirling over the lubricated knob as though his glans were a bomb-release trigger. "Jake, it sure doesn't feel to me like you have any problem." She whispered more hotly, her breath sultry and sweet from the drink. "This is one big hard *cock* I've got here in my hand! Let me take care of it for you. I want to do something for you, you know…for earlier."

His chest felt so tight he could barely breathe. "In a minute, I'll lose it…"

"Yeah?" She didn't sound convinced. She brought her thumb and forefinger together, and slid the ring slowly up and down, the pre-come pouring now. There was so much anyone would have thought his penis had been drenched in baby oil. "Relax, you're just nervous. Look, the barmaid's going back for ice!"

Flood didn't even bother to look.

"I know you're gonna come, I know you are," she insisted. "Get it. Come all over my hand…"

Flood kept his eyes closed. This was another oddity—his erections *never* lasted this long, save for last night during the beating. But there was no beating here, no violence, just perfect, unselfish lust. Perhaps his affliction was wearing off after so many years. *Oh, God, I can only hope…* If the Devil was sitting on the next stool, Flood knew he'd sell his soul just to come.

Her strokes quickened. Flood filled his mind with images of her: her hairless pussy in his face, his cock sliding between the consummate tits. He imagined the taste of her as his tongue spun circles over the clitoral nugget. He could imagine her own tongue cradling the back of each testicle like a spoon cradling an egg.

"Get it, get it. Let it all come out…"

Then the image ruptured. It wasn't his cock anymore on the verge of eruption. It was some other man's. And it was Felicity's hand, not Carol's, and Felicity's voice maintaining the secret whisper, "Get it, get it, *shoot* it…"

Flood's erection died in her hand to total limpness.

She pulled her hand out, perplexed. After some silence, she said, "What happened? Was I doing it wrong?"

"No," his voice crunched like gravel being walked on. He regained his breath, humiliated. "What did you say earlier—your rates, I mean. Was it five hundred for an hour?"

"Yeah, but…I can't charge you anything for *that.* I wouldn't feel right."

At least she's got some real character in there somewhere, he thought. "No, I mean now." He glanced to make sure the barmaid was out of earshot. "I'll give you five hundred right now, just to listen to me. I just want to talk."

Before she could agree, he slipped five bills from his wallet and handed them to her beneath the counter.

"Wow, I—"

It was a lark, Flood knew. But what the hell? The only person he'd ever talked to about this was Dr. Untermann. Back in Seattle, and Seattle was a long way away.

"I want to tell you about this problem I have," he began.

"Okay. Sometimes it's good to talk about a problem with someone you don't know, and someone you'll probably never see again. It feels better afterwards, and sometimes a different perspective helps. An anonymous one. You can talk without worrying about what the other person might think of you."

"Yes," Flood said. "I'm hoping so, anyway. And I'll try not to bore you." Then he began: "I have a sexual dysfunction which my psychiatrist charmingly refers to as a thematic-erotic inversion with ejaculatory incompetence and sequent erectile failure. How's that for a diagnosis?"

"It's a mouthful, all right." She popped a shrimp in her mouth, then whispered, "But they have stuff for that now." Then she held up her wrist purse. "If you need a Viagra, I've got 'em."

"It doesn't work, none of that does." He tapped his temple. "It's all psychological. It's like a toggle-switch in my brain. When I'm with a woman, and it gets past a certain point, that sexual switch gets turned off, by a single image, a single memory."

"What memory?"

"My ex-wife. Even after three years, it's like sabotage."

"Do you still love her?"

"Yes, and I know that's ridiculous and illogical. She ruined me—lied, cheated, stole, and left me—but after all that, I know deep down, I'd take her back without thinking twice."

"Why?"

He gave an honest shrug. "Because she was the best sex of my life, and now I can never have that again. My psyche's still obsessed with her; it's not even a conscious thing, at least that's what my therapist has told me. And I believe it. What else can I believe?" Flood's eyes panned over the nearly nude breasts and pubis, all that erotic flesh showing through the net—one of the most erotic images of his life. His penis—and his heart—felt like dead meat. "It's like I'm being haunted," he dragged on, lowering his voice. "It doesn't matter what the circumstance is sexually. Whenever I'm with a woman, right at the moment before I'd…come…I lose my erection, and…no orgasm. As if, right then, right at the moment of *my pleasure,* the woman I'm with becomes my ex-wife, and all that anger and negativity shoots right into my head, and kills all sexual function."

Carol's eyes blinked as she thought. "Okay, so…what about…"

"Masturbation? Same thing. Whatever image is in my head…while I'm doing it—whatever beautiful, stimulating woman—changes into *her.* Felicity."

"Maybe there's something you don't really know about yourself," she suggested. "Have you tried to get it on with guys?"

Flood winced, shaking his head. "No, no, no. I've never been attracted to men, never."

"What about porn?"

"Tried it, doesn't work. Oh, I'll get hard, I'll get excited, but—"

"Right before you'd get off, you lose it."

"Yes," he groaned. His heart had picked up while he'd been telling her, his blood-pressure shooting up. Any reference to Felicity did that, it put him in a state of subdued terror. "Porn, call girls, oils, lubes, herbs, oysters, prescription drugs, even penis-pumps—" He was beginning to blush—"I've tried it all, and it all fails. That toggle gets turned off. Then—nothing."

More contemplation. She'd replaced her hand on his thigh, ran her tongue over her bottom lip as she thought. "Well, now that you've talked about it to someone else, maybe that unplugged the toggle. Let's try…" Her eyes darted off. Now the barmaid was conversing with a bus boy at the other end of the bar, chattering away. Before he could look back to Carol, her face was in his lap, his waistband hauled down. She suckled his balls in her mouth, one at a time, then slipped the deflated penis past her lips. She worked the limp meat like a milking-machine nozzle on a cow teat. When turgidity requited, the action became more dainty, her tongue-tip running slow, excruciating lines up and down the shaft, tracing the veins. She even seemed earnest when she stopped a moment and whispered, "Don't let her come into your head. Think about me," and then she commenced with what he could only guess was the finest act of fellatio ever performed in the history of human sexuality.

His mind felt squashed with images of her, and just when he would fill her mouth with the horrendous back-pressure of sperm—

Felicity fell into his head like a guillotine blade; an instant later, his penis was a tiny and pathetic strip of nerveless meat.

There was nothing to say, yet she smiled just the same and offered, "Jake, whatever this problem is of yours, I know you'll get over it in time."

Flood doubted it but he nodded anyway. He ordered another round of drinks in silence while she patted his thigh in a lost condolence. "And when you *do* get over it," she continued, "find that card, fly back here, and call me."

"I will," he said uselessly. Now it was all gone, any rapport that had been there previously. He drained half his beer in one slug, trying to think of small-talk, but a sudden encroacher saved him:

"Hi, guys!"

An unseen arm was around him, and what felt like a very firm and very large breast pressed against his back.

"Hi, Therese," Carol said.

Flood turned to face a stunning, bright-eyed girl with ember-red hair cut like a flyer's cap. Breasts even larger and more gravity-defying than Carol's gaped back at Flood, jutting from a spritey, lissome pixie. A see-through white sarong and veil flowed off her hips and shoulders—a sun-ghost. Her skin, eyes, and smile radiated a cast of perfect health and vitality. *Sure as hell doesn't look like the prescription-dope junkie Leon was talking about,* Flood surmised. She leaned over and gave Carol a peck on the cheek.

"Therese, this is my friend, Jake. He saved me

from the grossest scumbag earlier—yeck! You should've seen this guy. But Jake whipped his ass."

"Defender of Women!" Therese exclaimed, then it was Jake's cheek that got pecked.

This is fucking killing me, Flood thought.

Therese was petite and short, and would've been shorter were it not for the heavily-soled beach sandals that elevated her. She lowered her face between the two of them, grinned impishly. "So are we doing a threeway, or what? I'm so horny I'm starting to show through my thong! Look, Jake—" and she squeezed next to him and pulled her thong down beneath the bartop. Flood's eyes roved down the flat belly to see that what she revealed: an adorable little toy of a pussy, dusted by the lightest red fur. The meticulous cleft below glistened.

"She's such a bad girl, Jake—and I mean sometimes she's *really* bad," Carol giggled. Then, to Therese: "Put that away!"

Both girls laughed; Therese repositioned the thong, then patted the adhesive triangle of fabric.

Flood ordered another round of drinks, testicles tingly. *Yes. This is definitely fucking killing me...*

"Jake and I just did some business," Carol sort of lied. "Now we're just talking."

"Oh. That's cool. Sorry I missed the fun. Maybe next time?" She gave Flood's tortured crotch a finger-tickling squeeze.

"Sure," Flood answered and drank more.

He was grateful that the next few minutes of banter didn't regard any manner of sex—just enlivened chit-chat. He *wasn't* necessarily grateful for Carol's hand on one thigh and Therese's on the other. Flood slowly grew erect again, painstakingly so, and at this point—the futility of it all now burying him as if in a hole—he felt as though an abstract bullet had been put through his head. Flood was the diabetic working in the Godiva chocolate factory; the Olympic swimmer standing in the middle of the Sahara Desert. So he drank gluttonously, pretending to listen to the girls' chat but hoping that enough alcohol would deaden his sexual nerves.

"Well, I better get going now," Carol said. "Thanks for everything, Jake. It was great hanging out with you."

Flood took a last useless look at the perfect breasts suspended in the big fishnet cups. "Likewise."

Therese gave his thigh another squeeze. "Where are you staying, Jake?"

"The Rosamilia Hotel, just up the beach."

Her breasts jiggled flawlessly when she stood up. "Cool. That's where I'm staying too."

"Maybe we'll run into you before you leave," Carol offered.

Flood was done talking, done thinking, and very much *done* with seeing what he couldn't have. "That'd be great," he said for formality. "You girls have a great day."

"'Bye."

"'Bye!"

Two more pecks on the cheek (and a final insufferable crotch-rub from Therese), and they were off. It was relief from the humiliation that overwhelmed

Flood when they left. Their shadows lengthened to sultry jet-black threads as they departed back to the sand.

His head droned with an arid silence, noise that wasn't noise. The sound of his soul? Because that's what his soul felt like just then. Arid, sterile. A husk.

It occurred to him that if he died at that very moment…he wouldn't have cared in the least.

«« — »»

His hangover dragged through the dinner hour and on into the night. He didn't bother checking in with Farris and Nathans to see how the day's business went; he didn't care. He lay naked and dried out on the hotel bed, head thumping, sparks of pain behind his eyes, throbbing along with the images of those two impeccable women: the abundant flesh of Carol's breasts blaring through the fishnets, the sparse mist of downy red hair covering Therese's mound. The coltish legs and flat abdomens. Each image twinged in his head with his heartbeat, and each heartbeat made him feel more hopeless. He thought of calling Dr. Untermann and telling her he felt like maybe committing suicide but didn't for two reasons.

One: *She'd think I was even more pathetic than I really am.*

And, two: *I don't have the balls.*

The sun had set brilliantly—a fireball that looked nuclear—and soon full dark bled into the room. Flood stared at the ceiling, not listening to the baseball game that shot scatters of wavering light on one wall. He wished he could fall asleep, erase the humiliating day, and begin a new man in the morning.

But he *wouldn't* be a new man, would he?

He'd be the same impotent, royally-fucked-up-in-the-head man he was today and had been for the last three years.

As his senses began to drift, he heard voices…

"It ain't bad really, we're doing better than the rest. We got fifteen girls and only a handful went bad. I'm sure Jinny won't fuck us over again. I think the skinny bitch learned her lesson."

Flood sat up in bed, glanced to his window. It was Oscar's voice, the big bad bald guy. *I left the window open,* Flood realized. The curtains billowed at a breeze. And the maids hadn't come in because he'd left out the do-not-disturb sign.

Flood sprang out of bed, seized, but not exactly knowing why. Just as he arrived to the window's edge, Leon's voice was floating up.

"I know. You're one terrifying motherfucker, Osc. Jinny'll have nightmares about you." A laugh.

"Bitch sucked my balls the whole time I was driving her home, then begged me to fuck her in the ass back at her joint."

A darker resolve shifted into Leon's next words. "But the other two are liabilities."

The other two? Flood recited.

"I had dinner with Therese tonight. Cunt lied to my face all through her steak. Got no idea Stoolie's ratting on Phipps' stable."

"You're shitting me?"

"Nope."

A pause drifted in with the warm breeze. Oscar said, "Lemme kill her. I've always hated the bitch."

Flood's heart stilled. He felt frozen, half his face peering out his window down into the window of Room 415. He could see the salmon-pink drapes fluttering, and in their gap, the brightly lit room. Oscar sat on the bed drinking a Heineken; Flood could see his knees and the back of his large, shaven head. Leon sat in the chair along the wall, legs crossed.

"I don't want her iced, but I want her uglied up bad for when we boot her lying ass back to Phipps."

The back of Oscar's bald head nodded.

"It's that other lying cunt I want iced," Leon added.

"Good. It'd be a pleasure."

Now Flood's heart surged, a lump of muscle that felt on the verge of bursting. The other one? *No!* he thought. *Not Carol!*

Who was the *other* one?

"I'm not sure where she is tonight," Leon continued. "I already talked to Nick. He's going to keep an eye out for her."

"Nick? Oh, yeah, the new security guy downstairs."

"I'm paying him well. He'll give me a call on my cell if he sees her."

WHO ARE THEY TALKING ABOUT? Flood's mind detonated.

But Carol had given him his card; she worked

directly for Phipps, not Leon. *If she was two-timing on Leon, she'd have Leon's card, wouldn't she?* he reasoned.

It didn't matter. Nothing would happen to either girl because Flood was going to make an anonymous tip to the police right now. Last night was a mistake, a weakness on his part.

And that won't happen again, he vowed.

It amazed him how the sound from their window carried so well up here. He could even hear the knock on their door.

"That's her," Leon said.

Oscar got up and walked out of the frame.

Flood stood shivering. He watched, unblinking, as Therese walked into a corner of the window. "Hi, guys!" she greeted. "Got a beer or something?"

Oscar handed her one.

"And I'll need a vykie for later. I'll cut it in half and use the rest tomorrow."

"No problem, babe."

"Oh, and look!" she exclaimed, all bouncy and bubbling and probably really high. She shoved some money at Leon. "Four hundred!"

"Thank you, Therese. You're a dear."

Flood could see her in the veil-like wrap she'd been wearing at the bar, her sleek back to the window, her short, bright-scarlet hair. Her rump looked naked due to the t-back, a perfect double-orb of flesh.

"I got some time," she said, but she seemed jittery now, overstrung. Was it the dope, or was she starting to think something might be wrong? "Got two doctors said they'll meet me at midnight for a double blowjob, said they'd pay five bills. You guys wanna fuck me first? I'm dying for some cock." A giggle, then, that sounded nervous. "I been so horny all day I been fingering myself whenever I've been sitting at a table."

"Yeah, I could use some of that," Leon said.

She shed the veil, then flicked off the t-back and bra. It seemed so perfunctory when she turned for the bed, but an instant later her breasts were suddenly tremoring. Her eyes bulged above Leon's opened hand, which had snapped around and clamped over her mouth. "Not too hard," Leon said very calmly. "Just put her lights out..."

WHAP!

Oscar, having already slipped on one of the sand-mitts, clouted her solidly once in the forehead. She fell limp as a sack of packing peanuts in Leon's arms. He tossed her on the bed—

—while Flood...watched.

His hand remained poised in mid-air—just like last night—about to reach for the phone. But instead—

Call. The. Police...

—he watched.

Oscar wrapped some duct tape around her mouth, then dropped his slacks and straddled her chest. She lay totally unconscious, arms and legs askew, head lolled to one side. Oscar spat liberally into the valley, then pressed the breasts tight around his penis and began to pump. Meanwhile, Leon had picked up one of Therese's inch-soled platform sandals, was fidgeting with it. "There we go, Osc," he said. He found some sort of clasp on the bottom of the sandal, then was peeling back the sole. "Stoolie wasn't jiving us."

"For the money you pay him to be our squeal, why would he?"

Inside the sandal there was some sort of a compartment, from which Leon withdrew a roll of cash. "Damn it, Osc. Bitch was hiding twelve hundred bucks in here. *My* money."

Oscar humped the slick crevice between Therese's bulging breasts, his hairy ass pistoning back and forth with the precision of a derrick. "And she was gonna leave here tomorrow and give it all to that white nigger Henry Phipps."

Leon was not offended by the "n"-word. "This shit hurts, man. I treat these girls right. What is it about that goddamn Phipps that has my bitches handin' him their money like he's Snoop Dog and Tupac combined?"

Oscar's answer was forestalled for his orgasm, which looped into Therese's still face. When he began talking again, he was wringing the last of it out of his cock like water out of a dishrag. "It ain't him, Leon. Wanna know what it is?"

"Tell me, my man."

"It's you. You're too nice to these bitches. You *let 'em* walk on you. If there's a buck to be made, these girls'll eat cum out of an ass-crack like a kid eating icing off a cupcake. Only thing white-trash like this respects is a Mack-Daddy who means business, a hard fuckin' hand, man."

"You know, Osc? You're right. It don't make sense, but you're right. And this is one hand that's gonna get real hard, real fast. But it just hurts, ya know?"

"Don't worry about it." Oscar was pulling his pants back up. "It ain't no big deal in the long run anyway. Any crew's gotta couple bad girls. We're weeding ours out." Oscar paused, extended a hand to the still-unconscious Therese. "You wanna piece of this before I start working on her?"

"No. She disgusts me."

And the entire scene disgusted Flood. He watched from his secret vantage point, hand still in the air to pick up the phone. His most sophisticated human senses felt severed, leaving only a blazing, mindless lust. His penis throbbed so hard it hurt, erect now beyond any maximum he'd ever experienced. Only the barest filament left of his spirit remained bellowing at him to call the police as, below, Oscar re-donned his sand-mitt and re-straddled Therese's chest.

"Remember, don't kill her," Leon instructed. "But I want that pretty little face of hers fucked up royally. When Phipps takes his first look at her, I want him to puke."

WHAP! came the first blow, which most certainly crushed her nose. Four more to either side just as certainly shattered her cheekbones and jaw. In only a matter of seconds, her face more resembled a busted jelly donut than a human visage.

It was as though Flood's skin had been nailed to the wall and he was pulling that skin through the nailheads when he finally managed to drag himself away from the window to the desk with the phone. Only three steps but in those three steps the hardest erection of his life went utterly limp.

Then that last filament of humanity made its exit.

If anything, his cock grew even harder when he stepped back to the window, a tethered animal with rabies, just about to break its chain. Flood knew then that he had no choice at this point…

He was masturbating at the window, sweat pouring. Oscar had already popped Therese hard over each eye, turning them to blue-black puffs of flesh. And now—

WHAP! WHAP! WHAP!

He was belly-punching her, his stout arm piledriving straight down with each blow. Bulbous breasts jounced with each slug.

Flood's climax burst, releasing the mental stopper on the day's agonizing back-up of semen. Like last night, it flew out the window in what seemed several yard-long strings. And like last night, there'd been not an inkling of any last-second sabotaging image of Felicity. His orgasm unwound as a celebration, bringing tears to his eyes. He staggered back when it was finally all gone, his loins buzzing. His cock felt content as a beast that had just fed gluttonously.

When he regained some order of sense, he found himself looking back down.

Please, God. Let them be done…

Oscar and Leon *weren't* done.

The bald man hunkered low, in one hand an empty beer bottle, in the other a hammer.

"You said you wanted her fucked up. Well, *this'll* fuck her up bigtime."

Leon stood, a knuckle to his lips, contemplating. "No, no—"

"What? Going back to Mr. Nice Guy?"

"She could bleed to death, Osc. I don't want that. I know— Do like you did that one chick we had a couple years ago. Remember? That Gothy looking bitch who was trying to hustle our girls for some service in Key West."

"Oh, yeah! Balloon Pussy! Straight up." Oscar put the bottle and hammer away, then put the mitt back on. He pushed Therese's ankles back toward her head, where Leon then grabbed them and pulled them back further. Her ass spread; the flesh of her vagina bloomed forward.

Oscar slapped down hard against her bared loins with the mitt's open palm. Time and time again, as hard as a strong man could. Flood reeled, nauseated, but locked in place by the taunt of an instantaneous erection as turgid and insistent as the one his hand had relieved a minute ago. He squeezed it; it felt hard as a steel-tube covered with skin, lust and blood purpling its dome, the slit inflamed and glazed already. *Oh my God...*

Again, that blade severed his humanity. Now Oscar was punching down outright into Therese's sex, which was blacking and bluing and swelling before his eyes.

WHAP! WHAP! WHAP! WHAP! WHAP! WHAP!

And more.

"Lookit that," Oscar remarked, subtly impressed by the image of his handiwork. The majoras of Therese's vagina, indeed, had ballooned with swelling, and with that image the pressure of desire built up similarly in Flood's penis, backed by further semen straining to be released. Flood thought of a water balloon being slowly stepped on. The idea of calling the police, now, did not exist anywhere in his head. Flood masturbated frenetically, eyes locked below.

Oscar and Leon were chuckling at the image of Therese's ludicrously swollen sex.

"I can't help it, man," Oscar chuckled further, dropping his slacks again. "I've just *gotta* fuck this…"

Oscar banged away, for quite awhile, as Flood nearly jerked the skin off of his own cock. At the moment when he would normally lose everything— when the image of Therese would invert to Felicity— Flood bit down on his lip to stifle the shriek of his pleasure that surely would've echoed outside. The first spurt blew against the glass, several more landed in loops on the carpet. This second orgasm of the night felt heroin-like. He stood ridiculously, heart hammering, legs still spread and one arm bracing him against the window frame. Insensible, he looked down and saw an impossibly still-hard penis throbbing. The final string of semen dangled from the piss-slit. When he squeezed his balls, the erection involuntarily flexed, and hook-shotted the remaining sperm in an upward arch where it stuck to his chest like a piece of flung spaghetti.

"Not enough," Leon said, out of frame. "It's the tits that bother me now."

"What about 'em?" Oscar was pulling his pants up again, while Therese lay with her legs wishboned, her genitals a dark swell. "That's the best pair of tits in your stable."

Leon kept the contemplative finger to his lips. "Yeah, and that's the problem. I *paid* for them. Let Henry Phipps pay for the next pair."

"Sounds fair to me," Oscar chuckled and produced an ice pick.

Flood couldn't move, paralyzed by the combinant disgust of continuing to watch while his loins still buzzed in post-orgasm.

Oscar had obviously done work like this before. Under each of Therese's breasts, he quickly shivved the ice pick up several times, puncturing the implants. Then he lifted his leg and stepped on each breast, deflating them. Multiple streams of red-tinted saline sprayed down Therese's lower body. A minute later, her state-of-the-art breasts were popped bags of skin.

"Much better," Leon said. "Let Phipps titty-fuck *that...*"

That was it for Flood. He almost lost his footing then, heels thumping backward until his knees gave out against the edge of the bed. Then he fell over on the mattress.

And lay there perfectly still.

He couldn't have gotten up again if he'd wanted to. But he could still hear them talking, ghost-voices fluttering around in the dark.

Leon: "Oh, yeah, that's a good job. This lying bitch is *hosed.*"

"Lemme get her ready."

"Right. I'll go down to the parking garage and bring the van around to the security door. I'll also have Nick come up and help you get her down the stairs. He'll lock all the stairwell doors on each floor so you can get her down without anyone seeing."

"Got'cha. That was fun. Wish we could be there when Phipps takes a look at what lyin' in his driveway in the morning."

Flood's heart felt truly dead.

"And it's a shame, too. Greed is what I mean. And the other one's worse. Taking a commission on any girl of mine she can swing over to Phipps. I can't be embarrassed like this, I can't have it. I can't have that gold-toothed piece of cracker shit laughing at me."

"You're talking about Ann now, ain't you?"

"Yes. You know what we have to do, right?"

"Sure."

"You have any problem with that?"

A chuckle. "Me? I groove on it."

"Excellent. Tomorrow, then. You pound that whore's face in till she's dead."

«« —»»

"Oh, Mr. Flood, our records show that you're booked for another night," the lanky hotel clerk observed at the desk.

"Yes," Flood mumbled. "Something came up; I've gotta leave a day early."

"Oh, okay. I hope you enjoyed your stay at the Rosamilia." The clerk produced a receipt, then Flood made a quick exit through the revolving door to the sun-lit entrance circle.

He couldn't leave till tomorrow, but there was no way he'd be staying the last night here. The place disgusted him, because it reminded him of what he'd done—or what he *hadn't* done—while Therese was being raped, beaten, and mutilated. It reminded him of what an utterly irredeemable human being he was...

The wheels of his suitcase squealed as he walked over to the next hotel. He knew what he *would* do, though; he simply hadn't done it yet and wasn't quite sure why. *Haven't worked up the nerve,* he supposed. *A coward all ways...* The procrastination, at least, gave him time for some lame rationalization. *I couldn't have called the police last night, because the call could be traced back to my room. Couldn't call from my cell phone, either—it's gotta be anonymous. And I couldn't call security 'cos that'd be even worse. Leon's got the hotel security man on his payroll.*

It worked a little, at least.

I'll call the police from a pay phone, blow the whistle on the shit going on in Room 415. I'll tell the cops about Jinny and Therese. Leon and Oscar will get questioned and spooked, not knowing who ratted on them. Maybe Jinny and Therese will even decide to press charges once the cat's out of the bag. I'll call Henry Phipps, too, from the card Carol gave me. The cops'll put major heat on everybody, and at the very

*least, Leon and Oscar won't beat up anymore girls,
and they sure as shit won't be killing this other girl
tonight.*

Flood sighed.

*Then I'll go back to Seattle and forget I ever
came to this awful beach...*

He stowed his bags at the new hotel, then made
it over to the convention center. Nathans and Farris
were exuberant; Flood had his sign-up meetings with
a flock of corporate buyers, and deals were sealed. It
took the rest of the afternoon but to Flood—with all
that guilt sitting on his shoulder—each meeting went
by in a fog. By dinnertime, he was done, and when
he went back out to the showroom, his associates
were high-fiving each other.

"This has to be our biggest haul at a con,"
Nathans was rubbing his hands together.

"You might be right," Flood said.

"We're making the west coast sales dickheads
look like doodly-squat," Farris added.

"Can't disagree with that, either," Flood said.
"You guys did great."

"Great enough for a night on the town—on the
company account?" Nathans pushed it.

"Once you guys get everything packed up..."
Flood gave him a company credit card, "yeah. Have
a good time."

"Thanks, boss! Won't you be joining us?"

"No, can't. But I'll see you guys at the airport in
the morning."

"Come on," Farris implored. "We'll hit some of
those kick-ass strip joints in Tampa."

The idea deadened the little left of Flood's soul.

"No, count me out, guys."

"He must have a hot date." Nathans grinned.

"Nope," Flood assured. "But I've got a very important call to make."

Flood left them in the convention's decaying buzz. He knew what he had to do, and he knew he *was* going to do it this time. The anonymity of the call would guarantee his protection; there'd be no way Leon or Oscar could come calling for him because they'd have no idea who made the call. The police would have to follow up on something this severe…

The phone coves were all full, sellers either reporting windfall sales to their home-bases, or a dismal turnout. Flood wasn't thwarted; he simply crossed the street back to the Rosamilia but when he found their phone cove full too, he saw no harm in putting off the call a while longer for some dinner.

He ate light and tried to relax, feeling better at least for knowing that he would soon report Leon's crimes, however late. He couldn't blame himself entirely, could he? Getting beaten up by your pimp was a hazard of any prostitute's calling.

Flood even recognized that these mental observations were indeed excuses, but that was okay now because he was going to stop it all.

And the time is now…

He left the restaurant and went straight to the phone cove where there were plenty of available phones. He sat in the first booth, lit a cigarette in spite of the NO SMOKING sign, and took some time to think. *And there's another girl named Ann,* he could tell the police. *When they find her, they're going to kill her.* Then he'd hang up and leave.

Easy.

But before he could dial, another voice leaked in through the gap in the booth's folding door, a woman's.

"Hey, Jimmy, this is Ann. Remember me? Yeah, yeah, two nights ago at the Swigwam. You said I could give you a call. Still game for tonight?"

Flood sat frozen, listening.

Ann...

Something moved then at the fringes of his vision. He didn't quite catch it.

Figures entering the cove?

A tap, not at his door but at the next.

"Okay, Jimmy, look, lemme call you back in a few, okay? Something just came up." A girlish chuckle. "Yeah, yeah, that too. Talk to ya real soon—'bye."

"There she is," a man's voice could be heard.

Another man's: "We've been looking all over for you, we were worried."

"I told you I'd be here, Leon. And here I am."

Leon and obviously Oscar.

"Good," Leon said. "I got a rich as hell optometrist wanting you in a bad way, showed him your pic in the brochure. But he's only got an hour, and his wife's in his room."

"That's cool. How about I use your room?"

"Great. Here're the keys. Go get ready, and we'll bring him up. He's going to meet us in the bar in a few minutes."

"Sure thing. I'll call you on your cell when he's done." Then the door in the next booth closed, and a woman walked by.

Flood's mouth locked open.

It was Carol.

She sauntered by, jingling keys in her hand.

When she was gone, the men talked further.

Oscar: "She ain't on to us."

"Yeah, the bitch is so arrogant, thinks she can get over on anyone."

"Never even knew her real name was Ann. Guess that's what she goes by when she's working behind my back for Phipps. Ain't that some shit?"

"Yeah, well. She's got a new name now: dead meat."

"Let's have a drink in the bar, then go up."

"Fine by me. Man, I can't wait to punch this bitch's ticket…"

Still as a stone, Flood remained in the booth. Leon and Oscar walked out of the cove.

They're going to do it, Flood's thoughts grated like ratchets. *They're going to be killing Carol in a few minutes…*

The phone felt melted in his hand. The numbers on the buttons blurred in his vision, and as his shaking index finger trembled forward, a sound like distant turbine filled his head.

Wait a minute…

Flood never dialed. He got a better idea instead. He left the phone hanging and walked out of the booth. A spit-and-polish concierge smiled stiffly when Flood approached. "How may I be of service, sir?"

"Where's the nearest Bank of America? I've got an emergency."

The concierge pointed toward the front. "There's one right across the street..."

«« —»»

Flood stared at the metal numbers: 415.

He gulped once, then knocked.

The low voices inside ceased when his knuckles rapped against the door. *Leon's probably looking through the peephole right now,* Flood deduced with a scared smile. He didn't give a shit anymore. He knocked again, then held his cell phone up before the peephole. "Open up or I'm calling the cops..."

The door to Room 415 clicked, then yawned open.

Flood wasn't surprised when he stepped in and found Oscar's pistol to his head. "Easy, pal. I've got business to discuss. And don't shit a brick. I know you're about to kill the girl."

Oscar glared in silent rage, his bald pate nearly quivering. He shoved Flood into the main room where Leon stood.

"He says he knows about Carol," Oscar said. "What the fuck's going on?"

Leon gaped at Flood. "You..."

Flood surrendered his cell phone to Oscar, then nodded to Leon. "You remember me. From the elevator?"

"Jack... Flood?"

"Makes sense you'd remember faces and names, you being a pimp and all—"

Leon was aghast. "Oscar, who *is* this guy? Why is he here?"

"I'm here to talk business," Flood began, smiling in spite of an effusion of sweat. "Of course, you guys can kill me right now, and no one would know."

"Oh, we can kill you, all right," Oscar began.

"Right, and you'd be stupid, which is par for the course so far." Flood noticed a closed door behind them. *That's the bedroom...* "First of all, you guys talk way too loud. I overheard several of your conversations in the phone cove downstairs." He pointed to the closed door. "And there's a couple-inch gap between those pink curtains in there. You both are about as sharp as Oscar's head."

Leon and Oscar remained stiff where they stood.

"I saw you beat up Jinny two nights ago," Flood finished. "And I saw what you did to Therese last night. You guys really take the cake for sick motherfuckers."

Leon's eyes bloomed toward Oscar. "I don't believe this shit, Oscar. What are we gonna do with this guy?"

"I got a couple ideas," Oscar said.

"Yeah, yeah," Flood chuckled. It was beyond him how he could be keeping his cool amid these killers. "Look, I know you got Carol in the bedroom—er, I guess her real name's Ann. I'd like to see her. What's the big deal? You guys got a gun on me. Let's go in there and talk business."

Leon's face remained stamped with disbelief. He nodded to Oscar, then they escorted Flood into the room.

Carol lay stretched naked over a shower curtain covering the bed, her ankles and wrists tied to the posts. Her eyes bugged above her gag. *God, she's beautiful,* Flood thought. The rotund, perfect implants quivered, her flat stomach sucking in and out in terror. Flood quailed when he noted the sand-mitts on the dresser, along with a cord and tourniquet, a manual drill, and a soldering iron.

Flood reserved comment. Instead he pointed to the gap in the salmon curtains. "See. At just the right angle, you can see in from outside."

"Bullshit," Leon muttered. "There ain't nothin' but the Gulf of fuckin' Mexico out there," but then he peeked out and up.

"The end-wing of the building," Floor said. "I was on the fifth floor. It was a million-to-one that the bed, the gap, and the vantage point all added up."

"Shit," Leon muttered and closed the curtains. He rubbed his face. "I still don't know what the fuck's going on. I can't *believe* this."

Flood chuckled again. "And I can't *believe* that Oscar hasn't frisked me yet. Shame on you, Osc. You're the bulldog, right? You're Leon's lieutenant. It's your job to protect The Man."

Oscar slammed Flood belly to wall and began to pat him down.

"Right and left jacket pockets, Osc…"

Oscar's face gaped like a kissing fish when he extracted five bands of $100 bills. "Holy fuck, Leon. There's a lot of fuckin' money here…"

"Fifty grand, Oscar," Flood told him. "I just got it out of the bank. It's for you guys."

Silence brewed like broth while Leon counted the money. His eyes seemed alight against the dark, shiny face. "Mr. Flood? To what do we own this excess of generosity?"

Without asking, Flood lit a cigarette while he tried to tame the nervous tremor in his hands. "I'm buying the girl," came his blunt reply. "Ann."

Leon was shaking his head. "Mr. Flood? This is quite unusual."

"Yeah," Oscar agreed.

"And I sense that you're a smart man…"

I'm a fucked up man, Flood almost chuckled. *Not necessarily a smart one.* "So are you, I hope. I think that handing fifty grand in cash over to you guys is proof of my good faith—"

Leon opened his mouth to talk but Flood cut him off.

"Let me have my say first, Leon, because you and I both know I could be dead a minute from now. You can keep the fifty grand and let the girl go, or…" Flood looked to Oscar. "Care to finish the sentence, Osc?"

Oscar smirked. "Or we can keep the fifty grand, kill the girl and kill you."

"Bingo," Flood said. "And you're thinking if you let her go, she'll go to the cops but, really guys, there's no evidence that any crimes have been committed here. She's a junkie and a prostitute. If you let her walk out that door, the only place she's gonna go is straight to the bus station. She'd be too afraid of you guys coming after her later." Flood turned his gaze. "Right, Leon?"

Leon looked back at him deadpan.

"And if you kill her *and* me," Flood continued, "you guys will never get the *other* fifty grand."

More silence stretched over the room. "What *other* fifty grand might this be?" Leon asked, tapping his Gucci'd foot.

Flood dragged his cigarette deep. "The other fifty grand I give you after the girl is out of here."

Oscar stepped forward. "It's on you?"

"Of course not, Einstein."

Oscar seemed duped by the remark. "Who's Ein—"

"Shut up, Oscar," Leon cut in. "Mr. Flood's got this thought out pretty well."

Flood chuckled out loud. "At least I hope so. Let the girl go, Leon. You've got nothing to lose."

Leon stroked his chin. "And fifty grand to gain, you say..."

"Right. How can I be bullshitting when I just handed you the first fifty?"

Leon sat down. The silk slacks hissed when he crossed his legs.

"I don't know about this, Leon," Oscar said.

Leon looked straight ahead when he said, "Oscar. Let her go."

Oscar's brow accordioned when he broke from his stance and cast a glance at Flood. He went to the bed then, and begrudgingly untied Carol aka Ann.

"You just won the lottery, cunt," he informed her.

The girl was vibrating when she faltered off the bed and pulled on her clothes. She'd obviously urinated, and all her skin looked pasty with fear-sweat. She stepped forward, then looked at Leon.

"Leave town," Leon said to her. "Mr. Flood here is correct. One way or another, one of my people will find you…"

The girl's hands shook so fierce she could barely get her dress back on. Her lower lip trembled. For an irreducible moment, she glanced to Flood…

Flood saw nothing but a wasteland in her eyes.

She grabbed her wrist-purse and scampered out of the room.

"Ain't that just like a bitch?" Oscar cracked a laugh, then slapped Flood hard on the back. "Didn't even say thank you!"

"It's my karma," Flood said through a thin smile.

But Leon wasn't smiling. He pressed his hands together and rested his chin on his fingertips, looking at Flood.

"Well, Mr. Flood? When will you enlighten us about this *other* fifty thousand?"

Flood lit another cigarette. "As soon as you guys finish packing…"

Flood sat in the seedy bathroom, the lights off. He'd left the door open a crack, which afforded him a perfect view of the bed. He arranged an ash tray on the rim of the filmy bathtub, and was actually sitting on the toilet seat lid.

Classy, he joked to himself.

The five-hour flight had passed like a barely recalled dream. The only reason Flood knew about the A-Top motel on Aurora Avenue was due to the

time he'd had to stay there overnight when a mud-
slide had blocked the highway from the Seattle airport. There were no better rooms to book unless he
wanted to drive all the way back to Sea-Tac. It was
the kind of place that had cockroaches but at least
the cockroaches were dead. $59.99 per night and
very remote. The parking lot was near empty, and
Flood had deliberately booked the farthest room in
the complex, so they could park in back.

He watched through the door crack, smoking.
Leon sat cross-legged on a rickety chair; he was
counting the second cash payment. The TV was
turned on, the sound turned down: a baseball game.

At the airport, Flood had rented an SUV for
Oscar. Then he drove Leon and himself to the motel
in his Cadillac Seville.

Risk, he thought baldly. Now that he'd given
them the rest of the money... *They could still kill me.*
Certainly. But Flood didn't think they would.

The sand-mitts lay on the dresser, along with a
cord and tourniquet, a manual drill, and a soldering
iron, plus pliers, a fileting knife, and some razor
blades...

Maybe I'm just like them, Flood suspected. *Or
maybe I'm far worse...*

That's when Oscar entered, with a very unconscious Felicity slung over his shoulder.

"No one saw a thing," the bald man bragged. "I
had her snatched two seconds after she came out of
the house..."

"Good work," Leon said.

Flood couldn't hear anything save for the drone

in his head, when he stood up in the dark and lowered his trousers. His penis was so hard it hurt.

"Let's get her tied down to the bed, and make sure the gag's tight," Leon advised. "Then wake her up and get to work."

Oscar chuckled, eyeing the implements on the night-stand. He plugged in the soldering gun.

Flood broke out in a sweat when he watched them strip the clothes off his ex-wife and lash her spread-eagled on the bed. His ecstacy made his blood seem scalding.

Flood had a feeling his cure was at hand.

AUTHOR'S AFTERWORD

I got the idea for this story one night while standing in a dark hotel room at about 4 a.m. This was four or five years ago. I'd taken a trusty Greyhound to Orlando in order to attend a Florida-writers book signing, and then I drank too many beers at an industrial club called Necropolis where publisher Dave Barnett moonlights as a DJ and enjoys the Life of Riley. I had a blast, even after realizing that I was twenty years older than almost everyone in the club, after which Dave treated me and others in his posse to a preeminently grease-laden breakfast at a seedy all-night diner. When I got back to my hotel room—Room 415—I discovered to my horror that it was a non-smoking room. So I did what all respectable smokers do in a non-smoking room. I smoked. I turned out all the lights and stood brazenly in my shorts before the window, which I opened as far as it would go (only a couple of inches. A "governor" was installed, presumably to thwart jumpers. Neat.) So I'm standing there smoking, at this wee hour, in the dark, when I look down and notice a window lit in a room one floor below and caddy-cornered against my vantage point. A several-inch gap existed between the salmon-colored curtains, and in the gap I could see a bed. And that's it.

I need to assure you all that the aforementioned is the ONLY aspect of this story rooted in truth. But as I was standing there watching my smoke siphon out my window, and periodically glancing down to the caddy-cornered window, Hitchcock's REAR WINDOW came to mind. "What if I saw someone get murdered in that window, right now?" I asked myself. "And what if it was a beautiful nude woman?" (Nudity seems to be an auxiliary ornament in most of my work.) Anyway, then I went to bed and awoke with a stunning hangover, and while Greyhounding back home the next day, all the details of the story were already in my head, with pretty much no conscious effort.

Very recently I read a Stephen King quote (in, I believe, the Cindy Margolis issue of *Playboy*—hubba-hubba) where King cited that he often gets story ideas simply from seeing a particular thing, after which the plot begins to create itself in his head. Though Mr. King's bank account and acclaim have precious little in common with mine, I was enthused to discover this singular commonality: I regularly get entire story ideas that originated by my witnessing some "thing." House, car, road, person, sound, etc. or some other essentially non-descript thingamajig that for some reason fires a subconscious creative spark. Most of the flesh in my novel THE BACKWOODS, for instance, was rooted in my glimpsing a 17-year locust through the window of a cab taking me to BWI airport in Maryland. A house right across the street from my wonderfully squalid apartment proved the initial fuel for FLESH GOTHIC (because the house is actually an office for a porno company. I live in a classy town.) The major plot device in the novella I'm writing now, MINOTAURESS (a prequel to THE HORN-CRANKER), was incited decades ago when I was a security guard inspecting an unoccupied two-story house. I was checking the locks of this supposedly untenanted dwelling when I heard a toilet flush upstairs. Ooo. Creepy. After possibly peeing my security pants in terror, I envisioned a *monster* sitting on the upstairs toilet. (The flusher, I'm happy to say, wasn't a monster, it was another security guard I didn't know was inside.) And in the case of this story—"Room 415"—it was something as simple as a hotel window that would hand me the entire plot and character line. This is *my* reason for cringing when asked that most clichéd question: "Where do you get your ideas?" It takes too damn long to explain and is actually quite unremarkable.

Afterwords are often unnecessary, and even more often boring, yet due to a publishing intricacy, I feel the situation warrants a tad more verbosity from Edward Lee. When Necro Publications began production on their excellent DAMNED Anthology, the publisher teamed up with Tampa's Camelot Books to jointly produce a super-fancy (and super pricey) "deluxe" edition for hardcore collectors. Only thirteen copies of this deluxe edition would be sold, and to enhance its uniqueness, I was contracted to write a story that would be exclusive to that edition. The story was "Room 415," but with a condition: that I could publish an alternate version later. When I was writing the piece, two different endings immediately occurred to me. One ending—a longer one—was what I'd call more commercial yet very negative, while the other ending was downright nihilistic. The latter ending wound up being the one I wrote for the deluxe inclusion. My favorite ending, however, is the one you've just read. While it's by no means a "happy" ending, it's not as dark and soul-dead as the deluxe. Why, then, is this my favorite? I think because I may be turning into a candyass as I get older. A wimp, but a happy wimp no less.

So. It seems that I've just penned about a thousand words to explain what would've sufficed with two sentences. Ah, the economy of language, and the disciplined skill of the true artist! I'm nearing the three-million-published-words point in my jubilant and unseemly career so, really, what's an extra thousand? This only to assure those thirteen hardcore souls who laid down serious coin that the version of "Room 415" in their deluxe does indeed remain exclusive. And as for those of you who've purchased this version, thank you. It's a story I like very much, and I hope you do too.

Edward Lee
St. Pete Beach, Florida
November 1, 2006

Edward Lee has had over twenty-seven books published in the horror and suspense field, including FLESH GOTHIC, MESSENGER and CITY INFERNAL. He is a Bram Stoker award nominee, and his short stories have appeared in over a dozen mass-market anthologies, including THE BEST AMERICAN MYSTERY STORIES OF 2000, Pocket's HOT BLOOD series, and the award-wining 999. Translation rights to several of his novels have recently been sold to Germany and Spain. His movie, HEADER, was filmed in late-2003 and awaits release. Meanwhile, CITY INFERNAL, MES-SENGER, and FAMILY TRADITION have been optioned for film. Lee lives on Florida's St. Pete Beach.